APPLE PIE AND TROUBLE

A SANDY BAY COZY MYSTERY

AMBER CREWES

A SANDY BAY COZY MYSTERY

MYSTERY

BOOK ONE

"Good morning, Meghan Truman! It's a beautiful day to be in Sandy Bay."

Meghan smiled sleepily at Karen, her seventy-two-year-old friend and former neighbor, who had just walked through the front door of the bakery, *Truly Sweet*. The two had met back in Los Angeles; Karen was a retired nurse, and she and Meghan had lived in the same apartment complex. Meghan adored Karen's enthusiasm and vigor, and Karen was filled with energy as she burst through the door.

"Someone's cheerful this morning." she said, rubbing her hazel eyes and stifling a yawn as Karen hoisted herself up to sit on the counter. "I wasn't expecting you. I'm sorry I'm still in my pajamas."

Karen tossed her frosted, shoulder-length blonde hair behind her shoulder and shook her head. "Sorry to surprise you, sweetie. I just couldn't resist stopping by. I was driving by after leaving the gym, and I saw that you had painted the front door. I just *had* to stop by and admire it."

Meghan grinned. "I couldn't sleep last night, and so there

I was, outside, painting the front door at two in the morning. I just wanted everything to be perfect, Karen. It's not every day that you start the business of your dreams."

Karen's eyes became solemn and as she nodded, Meghan saw her eyes begin to glitter with tears. "Meghan," she said. "I'm just so proud of you. At twenty-seven years old, you've moved across the country, and now, you're about to open your bakery. How fabulous!"

Meghan walked over to Karen and wrapped her arms around the older woman, feeling the warmth of her body as she leaned her head on Karen's shoulder. "You are too much. I wouldn't be here in Sandy Bay without your help; if you hadn't convinced me to leave LA, I would probably still be at some audition, still trying to make it as an actress."

Karen shrugged her narrow, but muscular shoulders as she gently pulled away from Meghan's embrace. "Look, sweetie," she said kindly. "You are young and beautiful, and the world is your oyster right now. Hollywood is a rough town for such a sweet girl. I think you'll be happier here than you've ever been. Sandy Bay is quiet, and the people are kind. The Pacific Northwest is a special place, Meghan, and I know you'll fit right in."

Meghan ran a hand through her dark, messy hair and sighed. She had another long, busy day ahead of her. After moving to Sandy Bay from Los Angeles on a whim three weeks ago, Meghan's life had been brimming with excitement; Karen had persuaded her to lease a charming little two-story brick building on the town square, and Meghan had applied for the permits to open Truly Sweet, the bakery of her dreams. She had moved her belongings into the tiny upstairs apartment above the bakery, and she had changed her address at the post office. After nearly three years of trying to make it in Hollywood, Meghan was now officially a resident of Sandy Bay, and as she painted and cleaned in preparation for the opening of her bakery, she felt herself begin to feel at ease for the first time since she had left home in Texas after college.

Karen lifted her arms above her body and stretched. "Meghan? Are you sure you don't want to go to pilates with me? There's an afternoon class today, and plenty of girls your age go. It could be a good chance to meet people in Sandy Bay."

Meghan raised one eyebrow at Karen and shook her head. "Karen," she began, "It's nice of you to ask me, but I have to tell you the same thing I told you when you first asked me last night. I've been moving boxes and painting for days, and my body is aching. I can hardly move, let alone do pilates."

Karen shrugged. "Just had to ask," she said. "Well, I'll let you wake up a bit and get your day started. I just had to compliment you on the front door. The yellow paint looks simply fabulous."

Karen leaned in to kiss Meghan on the cheek, and then she marched out of the bakery, her matching velour sweatsuit lighting up the gray morning as she strode to her orange jeep.

"That lady is in better shape than *me*, and I'm half her age." Meghan murmured to herself as she looked down at her curvy, womanly figure. "I hope I have that much energy when I am in my seventies, because I definitely don't have any today."

Meghan slowly made her way upstairs to change into her clothes, her legs and arms sore from the labor she had put into making Truly Sweet beautiful. As she came back downstairs, she grinned as she stepped into the bakery. She was proud of her hard work; she had little experience with decor or design, but with Karen's help, she had turned the dilapidated brick building into a quaint little space. The walls were painted pale yellow, and little white tables were positioned around the dining area. The counters and cabinets were painted white as well, and a long, painted wooden shelf held a diverse array of rich, green succulents that gave the room a fresh, airy feeling.

"It's almost ready," Meghan said, as she stood in the bakery, her hands on her hips. "It's almost *my* time to shine!"

Meghan took a long breath as she surveyed the pale yellow walls of the bakery. "These could use another coat of paint," she muttered to herself, inhaling deeply. "I could probably get away with the walls as they are, but another coat would be just perfect. We only have three days until the opening though...."

Meghan took a seat at one of the little white tables and looked around the room. She had poured herself into making Truly Sweet a lovely place, and she hoped the citizens of Sandy Bay would be pleased by the addition of a bakery. Back in Los Angeles, Karen had sworn to Meghan that opening a bakery in Sandy Bay would be a wonderful idea, and now, with only a few days until the grand opening, Meghan felt her heart flutter with nerves each time she imagined someone stepping inside and having a taste of Meghan's homemade treats.

"It'll be *awesome*, Meghan. Just imagine it!" Karen had gushed back in California. "Sweetie, you've been auditioning nonstop for every movie, play, and commercial, and I can see it in your eyes that you're unhappy. You always talk about that bakery you worked at in your hometown as a girl, and I see the way your face lights up when you bring a new little dessert over to show me. I'm moving home to Sandy Bay at the end of the month. Come with me. There's a cute little building downtown that's been sitting vacant, and *you* could start a new chapter with a bakery. Just imagine!"

Meghan thought back to that conversation with Karen. It felt like ages ago, but in reality, she had only been in Sandy Bay for a few weeks. Meghan was nervous about the bakery's opening ceremony, but as she studied the little space she had devoted herself to fixing up, she felt her heart pound with pride.

"It's going to be great," she whispered. "I've loved making this place pretty, and if it weren't for Karen, I would still be back trying to make it big in LA. This is where I belong now. This is going to be *home*."

A loud pounding at the front door of the bakery stirred Meghan from her wistful daydreaming, and she nearly jumped out of her seat.

"Hello?" she called out. "Who is it?"

"This is Norman Butcher! Who are *you*?"

Meghan cringed at the loud, fussy voice on the other side of her newly painted door. She rose from the chair and tucked her dark hair behind her ears.

"It's Meghan. Meghan Truman? I'm new in town."

Meghan carefully pulled the white lace curtains back and peered outside. A short, stout man wearing a pair of tortoise-shell spectacles looked back at her, and he gestured feverishly toward the door.

"Please, open this door. We need to have a chat, Ms. Truman."

Meghan noticed a British accent. She opened the door, and the man came barreling in.

"I see from the sign that was put up outside that this is a bakery," he said brusquely as he took a seat in one of the little white chairs. "I own a tea shop just across the way, and we bake and sell our own goods."

Meghan joined Norman at the table. "Another business owner? How nice of you to stop by." she said happily.

Norman shook his head vigorously. "This isn't a social call," he said sternly as Meghan's eyes widened. "You're new in town, and when I saw that someone was trying to open a bakery here, I knew I needed to speak up."

Meghan shook her head. "I'm not trying to open a bakery here," she said steadily, folding her hands delicately in front of her on the table. "I *am* opening a bakery here. I have all the paperwork and permits ready, and as soon as I'm finished fixing this place up, I'll be in business."

Norman folded his arms across his chest. He was an older gentleman, and as he furrowed his brow, the wrinkles on his forehead cut deep across his face to form an angry expression. "Look," he whispered as Meghan leaned away from him. "This town doesn't *need* another place to buy baked goods. It could be years before your business makes a profit. You look young enough. Why don't you go somewhere else and open a bakery? I hear Nantucket is nice."

Meghan rose from the table, irritated with Norman's intrusion. She had work to do, and he was being quite rude.

"Thank you for stopping by today, but I must say goodbye for now," she said, her hazel eyes filled with annoyance as she gestured toward the yellow door of Truly Sweet. "I'll be staying in Sandy Bay. I do hope we can get along well together."

Norman muttered under his breath as he stomped out, and as he stepped across the threshold, Meghan turned the lock on the door.

"That's *enough* excitement for one morning," she huffed, trying to lower her shoulders and relax her body. She was confused by Norman's visit; everyone she had met in Sandy Bay thus far had been so kind, but Norman's visit was perplexing. He had been terribly rude, and Meghan did her best to not get upset.

Turning back to face the kitchen, she shrugged. "Time to get back to work!" she exclaimed, picking up a paintbrush and smiling as she got underway. She wondered if there would be any other distractions that morning.

2

"**I**t just looks *fabulous*," Karen cooed as she looked around Truly Sweet.

Meghan beamed. It *did* look fabulous, and the grand opening of the bakery was proving to be a success. The night before, Karen and Meghan had hung strands of string lights through the wooden rafters in the ceiling of the dining area. The lights were twinkling, and the pale yellow walls glowed. Karen had loaned Meghan fifty antique powder blue plates to place on the white tables, and nearly fifty guests were milling about Truly Sweet.

"I couldn't have done it without you," Meghan said, reaching to hug Karen. "This night wouldn't have been possible without you."

Karen playfully rolled her eyes. "Nope. You get all the credit, sweetie. Now, go enjoy your special night. I need to go have a piece of that apple pie of yours! My niece, Debbie, is here, and she said it's the best thing she's ever eaten and that nearly all of it is gone already."

"You'll have to introduce us." Meghan said. "I'm happy she was able to come."

Karen smiled. "She's about your age. You two will get on well. I'll bring her over sometime this week. You go mix and mingle; you only have one opening ceremony, and I want you to soak it in."

Karen scuttled away, and Meghan's heart swelled with pride as she glanced around the room. People were smiling, her desserts were being eaten, and the opening ceremony was proving to be a roaring success! For the first time since she had arrived in Sandy Bay, Meghan truly felt as though she had made it and that everything was going to work out for her in her new home.

Within a week of the opening, Truly Sweet was one of the most popular establishments in town. Meghan was swarmed with orders and walk-in customers, and with every day, her schedule grew busier.

"I just don't know how I'll manage it all!" Meghan exclaimed to Karen on the phone one evening. "It's taken off faster than I ever imagined."

Meghan could hear Karen giggling. "I told you," she said gleefully. "I told you that this was a good idea."

"It was," Meghan agreed. "I just hope I can maintain it all."

"How about I stop by tomorrow and give you a hand?" Karen asked. "I have some time between my morning run and my yoga class. I can stop by and help you."

"That would be wonderful," Meghan said, thankful for Karen's unfailing support. "I can't wait to see you."

The next day, Karen visited the bakery in the afternoon. It had been a hectic morning, but all was quiet when Karen arrived, a young, blonde-haired woman walking in behind her.

"Karen!" Meghan said. "So happy to see you. It's been a crazy morning."

Karen looked at the pile of dishes in the sink, her eyes large. "I see that," she said. She walked behind the counter and retrieved a spare apron, tying it tightly around her thin waist. "I'll get to work on these dishes, but first, let me introduce my niece."

The blond woman stepped up to the counter and smiled at Meghan. "It's nice to meet you.

I was at the opening, but I didn't get to say hello. I'm Debbie. Aunt Karen speaks so highly of you."

Meghan studied Debbie, noticing her impeccable clothes and tidy appearance. Meghan felt sloppy and bashful; her dark hair was thrown up into a loose bun atop her head, and she was covered in flour from the morning in the kitchen.

"Thanks," Meghan said quietly, looking down at the ground. "Nice to meet you, Debbie."

Karen picked up the pile of dishes and carried them to the back room. "I'll work on these. You girls chat."

Meghan shifted awkwardly, but Debbie continued to smile at her. "The opening was so nice," Debbie said, smoothing her blunt, chin-length hair with the back of her right hand. "There is some serious potential here, Meghan."

Meghan felt herself relax, and she smiled shyly at Debbie. "Thank you so much," she said, feeling herself blush.

"Seriously," Debbie continued, looking around the bakery with business-like ferocity. "I was going to be an investment banker on Wall Street. I'm back in town from New York as of last month. It just didn't work out. I know my stuff though, and from the looks of what you have going on here, I think that with the right management and systems in place, this place could be listed on the stock exchange."

Meghan's jaw dropped. "Really?" she asked, placing her hands on her hips, her eyes wide. "You really think that?"

Debbie bobbed her head up and down. "I do. I've seen a lot and I know a lot, and this place smells like success. I can just feel it."

Meghan grinned. "Thank you for saying that," she told

Debbie. "That means so much. I opened this place to do something I enjoyed and to serve the people of Sandy Bay. If I'm even a local success, I'll be happy."

Debbie shook her head. "Forget local success, Meghan," she said matter-of-factly. "This place could expand as soon as next year. Like I said, I know potential when I see it. Anyway, I wanted to stop by and say hello. Aunt Karen has said so many nice things about you, and I wanted to let you know that if you're ever interested in talking about the finances of this place, I would love to have a chat over coffee."

Meghan beamed. "I might just take you up on that," she replied. "Thanks so much, Debbie!"

"Of course," she said, turning on her heel. "It's been a pleasure. Like I said, any time you want to talk, just let me know."

When Karen returned to the front of the bakery with the new-cleaned dishes, Meghan was still basking in the glow of Debbie's praise. "Your niece was so nice!" she gushed. "She thinks this place will be a success."

Karen nodded earnestly. "She knows her stuff. Debbie is a smart cookie, and if she thinks this place is going to be a hit, I have no doubt that Truly Sweet is going to grow more and more and more."

Karen's words proved prophetic; within two weeks of its grand opening, Truly Sweet had grown even more popular, and Meghan was in desperate need of assistance.

"What should I do?" she asked Karen over the phone one morning. "It isn't even nine yet, and I have too many orders. I can't handle this workload by myself, Karen."

"Hire someone. I hear Lori, at the tea shop, is looking for a new job."

Meghan gasped. "The tea shop? Norman Butcher's tea shop?"

"Yes! Have you been there?"

Meghan groaned. "Norman Butcher stopped by the bakery before the opening," she said, recalling the tense visit from the stout, elderly gentleman. "He seemed angry that I was opening a bakery."

"Oh, don't listen to Norman," she reassured Meghan. "Debbie tells me that he has been bad-mouthing your place all week, but clearly he isn't hurting your business."

"WHAT?" she gasped. "What did Debbie say?"

"Debbie said that Norman has been talking poorly about Truly Sweet, but I think it's funny," she said dismissively. "That grumpy old geyser can say whatever he wants, but if it's nine in the morning and you have too much work already, I think that his nasty words aren't doing a lot of harm. Don't think about him, Meghan. Think about your business. Think about talking to Lori. She's a sweet girl, and she would be a great addition."

"Thanks, Karen," Meghan said as she hung up the phone. Her stomach churned. Despite Karen's nonchalant feelings toward Norman's attitude, Meghan was very hurt and offended. What had she done to him to warrant such scorn? Feeling frustrated, she removed her apron. After the last walk-in customer left, she turned the OPEN sign to CLOSED and marched out of the bakery.

"I'm going to the tea shop right now," Meghan muttered to herself as she walked toward Norman's business. "I'm going to offer Lori a job and give that man a piece of my mind."

3

"And she said she would think about it. Norman wasn't even there, and Lori looked so pleased when I offered her the job." Meghan gushed to Karen as the two women sipped on cinnamon tea in the dining area of the bakery.

"That's fabulous!" Karen replied, her eyes bright with excitement. "Lori is such a good girl. She never really left town when she graduated from high school, and she's a little green, but I think the two of you will get along nicely. She's a hard worker; I remember when she was just a slip of a girl, she ran her own dog walking business. She worked all weekend walking dogs, and she'll surely be able to take some of the load off of you."

Meghan smiled. She had been furious as she walked over to Norman's tea shop, but her anger had quelled the instant she met Lori. Lori was tall and pretty, and Meghan guessed she was about twenty years old. Lori had a pixie cut that made her green eyes look enormous, and a smattering of sandy freckles across her cheeks. Her smile was genuine and warm, and it made Meghan feel hopeful that *something* good might come out of her tense relationship with Norman Butcher.

"What can I do for you?" Lori had chirped as Meghan walked into the tea shop.

"You're Lori, right?" Meghan asked.

"That's right. I'm Lori!" Lori's smile was huge, and her dimples cut deep into her freckled cheeks. "Do we know each other?"

Meghan shook her head. "We don't yet," she began. "But I hope we can get to know each other a bit better. I'm Meghan Truman. I moved to Sandy Bay from Los Angeles to open Truly Sweet, the bakery on the square."

Just then, a sturdy, muscular man walked past Meghan, his hat pulled down and his eyes fixed on the ground.

"Excuse me," the man said, walking out of the tea shop and into the afternoon sun. Meghan noticed streaks of dirt on his overalls as he left, and she could smell the unmistakable odor of an unwashed man. Meghan nearly gagged as the man passed her, but Lori was unfazed.

"Bye, Jamie!" she called out, her voice friendly as she waved goodbye. "Thanks for your help. I couldn't have fixed the sink by myself."

Lori turned her attention back to Meghan. "That was Jamie, the handyman in town. I am just useless when it comes to fixing things, and he was sweet enough to come over in a jiffy to help me with our leaky sink. Anyway, so sorry. What were you saying?"

Meghan brushed her hair off of her shoulders and smiled. "Truly Sweet. The new bakery?"

Lori's eyes sparkled. "Truly Sweet? Yes! I've walked by the shop a few times, and I just love what you've done with the place. I hear your apple pie is to die for."

Meghan couldn't help but to blush; she was thrilled that her little bakery was receiving such praise.

"Thank you so much," she said, tucking a lock of dark hair behind her ear. "I wanted to ask you something important, Lori. I'm swamped with work; I've never run a business before, and with all the orders coming in, I need some help. Karen Denton, one of my friends in town, mentioned that you might be looking for a new job, and I was wondering if you had any interest in working with me at the bakery?"

Lori's face grew pale, and the smile vanished from her lips. She looked left and right and put a finger to her lips.

"Shhhh," she whispered to Meghan. "The owner isn't around today, but I don't think this is something I should talk about here in the tea shop."

Meghan defiantly placed her hands on her hips. "You mean Norman Butcher? I hear he's been saying some unpleasant things about my bakery. If he's treating me, a stranger, that way, I can't imagine what it's like to work for him."

Lori looked down at her feet, her eyes filled with sadness. "Imagine what it's like to be his daughter…."

Meghan's mouth dropped open, but she quickly recovered her composure. "His daughter?" Meghan said, her eyes widening. "Do you mean…."

"Norman is my father. This is our family business." she said, her voice shaking. "I've worked here since I was a girl, and now I work here full time."

Meghan placed a hand over her mouth and took a long breath. Karen hadn't mentioned that Lori was Norman's *daughter*.

"You said that he said some nasty things to you? I'm so sorry. My father has been getting meaner and meaner lately, but I promise, it isn't personal. He treats everyone like that."

Meghan watched as Lori's eyes filled with tears. Feeling sorry for the young woman, Meghan reached out to take Lori's hand.

"I'm sorry to hear that," she said softly, trying to meet Lori's gaze. "I'm sorry he isn't nicer to you. You seem like a very nice girl, Lori, and you don't deserve that."

Lori began to cry, and Meghan squeezed her hand. "Lori, think about working for me," she said. "Truly Sweet is a wonderful place, and maybe some time away from your father would be good for you. Absence can make the heart grow fonder, and maybe if you two have some time apart, you'll be able to get along again."

Lori sniffled. "It would be nice to have some time apart. Our house is so small, and spending forty hours a week in this little tea shop makes it even more tense."

Meghan nodded, feeling as though she were getting somewhere with Lori. "Yes! See? Come work for me. I could even talk with your father about it. I had some things to say to him anyway, but this seems more important. Will you think about it?"

Lori wiped the tears from her cheeks and smiled weakly. "Yes," she said, running a hand through her short hair. "I'll think about it."

Later that day, Meghan was excited to share the news with Karen, but as the two chatted about Meghan's encounter with Lori, an unexpected visitor marched into the bakery.

"What do you think you're doing? How dare you try to steal my employee away?" Norman Butcher shouted, waving a finger in the air at Meghan as the remaining customers in the bakery got up and left.

"You mean your *daughter*?" she said calmly, though irritated that Norman had scared away customers. "I'm not trying to steal her away," she explained firmly as Norman glared at her. "I simply offered her a job. I have too much work for one person, and I need help."

Norman clenched his hands into fists and glowered at

Meghan. "You don't have any business trying to steal what's mine!"

Karen rose from her chair and wagged her finger at Norman. "Norman Butcher!" she said. "You are being fabulously rude. Meghan is new in town, and from what I hear, you've treated her terribly. Surely you have better manners than this."

Norman tightened his jaw, and Meghan could see the thick, purple veins in his forehead growing darker. "Surely *she* has better manners than to steal my employee!" he said, pointing at Meghan. "Lori works for *me*."

Karen rolled her eyes. "You've never treated that girl well, and everyone in Sandy Bay knows it. I had even forgotten she was your daughter because of the way you've acted toward her; I've been living in LA for the last few years, and when I was in the tea shop last week, the way you spoke to Lori was *unforgivable*!"

Norman rolled up his sleeves to reveal his pale, fleshy arms as if preparing for a fight. Karen did the same, and Meghan was impressed with the shape and definition of Karen's sculpted biceps.

"Norman," Meghan said quietly. "You've insulted me and you've insulted my business. I'm willing to let that go. I want to hire Lori to work here, and if she wants to, you can't stop me. Your tea shop was empty when I went in today, and I think Lori's talents could be of better use at Truly Sweet."

Norman's eyes narrowed. "Over my dead body," he said, turning on his heel and storming out of the bakery.

* * *

THE NEXT MORNING, the tiny silver bells on the front door chimed as Lori walked into the bakery.

"Lori!" Meghan exclaimed. "I'm so happy you stopped by. Have you come to accept my offer?"

Lori hung her head, and Meghan knew what her decision was.

"That's okay," she said, coming around from the back of the counter to hug Lori. "I enjoyed talking with you yesterday, Lori, and I hope that even if I can't have you as an employee, I can have you as a friend?"

Lori stepped back from the hug, and Meghan could see the weak smile on her face.

"I really wanted to work for you, but I can't. My father says I'm to have nothing to do with you," she said sadly. "He told me to stay away from here. I'm sorry he came by last night. He's horrible."

Meghan shook her head. "It's not your place to apologize for him," she said gently.

"Well, I'm still very sorry for him," Lori said. "I have to go now. He's working today, and he's expecting me soon."

"Don't leave just yet. Stay here a minute; I have something for you." Meghan said, dashing out of the front room. She soon returned with a large box. Lori's eyes widened.

"For me?" she asked as Meghan handed her the box. Meghan nodded.

Lori slowly opened the box. "It's an apple pie!" she squealed, her large eyes glittering. "Thank you, Meghan!"

Lori stuck a finger into the box and scooped out a tiny piece of the pie. She brought the morsel to her lips and closed her eyes, moaning in satisfaction.

"It really *is* to die for," she said as Meghan grinned in delight.

4

———————

"He's dead, and it's *your* fault!" Sally Sheridan shouted at Meghan, her brow furrowed and her hands shaking.

Sally, an elderly resident of Sandy Bay, also known as Sally Scary-den, or so Karen had told her, had marched into Truly Sweet in a rage only moments earlier. Meghan looked down at the wooden floor and bit the inside of her cheek, puzzled by this outburst from Sandy Bay's grumpiest elder stateswoman.

"I'm returning this pie, and I want a full refund! I already had diarrhea after consuming this trash, and after what happened to Norman Butcher, I want my money back *now*."

Meghan felt the color drain from her face. Mrs. Sheridan had thrown a Truly Sweet box with a half-eaten apple pie on the counter, and Meghan gasped as the remnants of the treat spilled all over the floor.

"Mrs. Sheridan!" she cried out, watching the gooey, brown pieces of pie soak the floor.

"Serves you right! You *killed* Norman Butcher. Everyone

in town knew he didn't like you, and you went and killed him off. I'm not surprised, either. You people from California think you can do whatever you want."

Meghan dropped to her knees and began to clean the floor. "I'm not even from California. I grew up in Texas," she whimpered, feeling hot, angry tears well in her eyes.

Mrs. Sheridan narrowed her eyes and tapped her cane on the wooden floor directly in front of Meghan.

"What are you *talking* about?" Meghan stammered, humiliated by Mrs. Sheridan's outburst and embarrassed that a paying customer had been made ill by her pie.

"I don't care *where* you are from, but I know where you are going. JAIL!" she shouted, turning and hobbling out of the bakery. "And don't think I won't be back for my refund."

Meghan stopped reaching for the pieces of the broken pie and sank down, resting her head on the floor of the bakery. She had been informed that Sally Sheridan had a reputation of being a difficult customer, but to insinuate someone's death to extract a refund seemed way below the belt. Sadly, cleaning the mess that Mrs. Sheridan had made would now be her top priority that morning.

Hours later, Meghan's stomach was still churning over the unpleasant visit from Sally Sheridan; she could not believe how rude Mrs. Sheridan had been. Needing some encouragement, Meghan picked up the phone to call Karen.

"Hello?"

Meghan winced as Debbie picked up the phone; she liked Debbie, but what she really wanted was one of Karen's famous pep talks.

"Meghan? What's up?" Debbie asked.

"Is Karen there?"

"She is swimming laps in the backyard; she's been going for nearly two hours now, but I can get her if you'd like?"

Meghan sighed. "No," she said. "Don't interrupt her. I'll call back."

"What's wrong? You sound upset."

"Well," she began. "I just had the strangest visit from Sally Sheridan. She came into Truly Sweet demanding a refund for an apple pie. She was saying strange things too about Norman Butcher? It was just so off, Debbie. She was so nasty, and I just don't know what to do."

"Meghan," Debbie said. "That lady is *known* for marching around Sandy Bay and trying to get money back. It's shameful. Totally embarrassing. Everyone hides when they see her coming, and it sounds like you're her latest victim."

"So it's not just me?" Meghan asked hopefully.

"No, absolutely *not*. Just ignore her. Sally Sheridan is such a cheapskate and would *kill* to get money back. Seriously. She would do *anything*."

"But she said Norman Butcher was…"

"Don't believe anything that woman says. It's pathetic. Anyway, hey, I have to let you go, but trust me, Meghan. Sally Sheridan is a nasty old bat, but her bark is *usually* worse than her bite…."

Meghan smiled, relieved to have some reassurance.

"Thanks, Debbie. You're the best."

"Anytime!"

The next day, Meghan was startled when a tall, handsome police officer stepped into the bakery.

"Good afternoon!" Meghan called out, her heart pounding quickly as she stared at the police officer. He looked to be about her age, and with his biceps nearly bursting out of his tight uniform, Meghan could feel herself blushing.

"Can I help you?" she asked, slowly lowering her eyelids and then glancing back up, a flirtatious move she had been trying to perfect for years.

The policeman shook his head. "Ma'am, are you Meghan Truman, owner of this establishment?"

Meghan nodded. The officer's voice was stern, and the smile disappeared from Meghan's lips as she looked up into his serious face.

"Yes? I'm Meghan. Why do you ask?"

The officer nodded curtly. "I'm Jack Irvin. I'm with the Sandy Bay Police Department. Ms. Truman, do you know a Mr. Norman Butcher?"

Meghan nodded. "Yes, I know Mr. Butcher. He's a nasty fellow. He came in here screaming at me this week. He's the meanest person I've met in Sandy Bay. Why? Why do you ask?"

"He's dead, Ms. Truman," Officer Irvin stated brusquely as Meghan's jaw dropped.

"What?" she gasped, her hands flying to her cheeks as the shock set in. "He's dead? He was just in here a few days ago. How horrible!"

The officer stared at Meghan, and she felt uncomfortable with his stony gaze. "Is there something else, Officer Irvin?" she asked. "What can I help you with? I didn't know Norman very well, but is there something you need?"

Officer Irvin nodded. "Ma'am," he began. "Mr. Butcher was discovered dead in the tea shop by his daughter, Lori Butcher. Ms. Butcher says he was cold and stiff, leading us to believe that he had been dead a while before she arrived. The cause of death was unclear until some reports were run a few hours ago, and we have good reason to believe that he was poisoned."

Meghan's eyes widened. "Poison?" she whispered. "That's awful! Poor Lori. Poor Norman."

Officer Irvin raised an eyebrow and stared into Meghan's eyes. "We have good reason to believe that *you* may have poisoned Mr. Butcher, Ms. Truman."

Meghan shrieked. "Me?" she cried in disbelief. "*Me*? Poison? What?"

"Witnesses say that you and Mr. Butcher have had several heated confrontations, including one yesterday. We've also been informed that you were attempting to hire one of his current employees, Ms. Lori Butcher, and that you were quite upset when Mr. Butcher refused to allow Lori to work for you."

Meghan shook her head vigorously. "I wasn't happy with Norman, and we had an argument about Lori yesterday, but that doesn't mean I would poison him! Where would you come up with that crazy idea?"

Officer Irvin jerked his chin at one of the fresh apple pies displayed on the counter. "The testing we've done on the body indicates that the only thing in Mr. Butcher's stomach was one of your apple pies. A *poisoned* apple pie, Ms. Truman."

Meghan gasped. "Poisoned? What? Officer, I had nothing to do with Norman's death! I sent a perfectly fine apple pie home with Lori yesterday when she stopped by. Have you talked with Lori?"

Officer Irvin placed a hand on the set of handcuffs dangling from his belt and looked at Meghan's trembling face. "Ms. Truman," he said. "We've spoken to Ms. Butcher, and she's confirmed that you expressed frustration with her father over the employment matter. I'm sorry to tell you, but you are our prime suspect behind Norman Butcher's murder. I'm going to need you to come down to the station with me for some questions. You might want to give your lawyer a call."

Now, three days after being interrogated, Meghan sat alone in the quiet aftermath of Sally Sheridan's visit to Truly Sweet. Everyone in Sandy Bay thought that she had killed Norman Butcher; between the confrontation they had had the night before his death, to the poisoned apple pie, the court of public opinion had ruled Meghan guilty as charged, and life would never be the same.

5

M eghan had been inconsolable on the drive over to the Sandy Bay Police Station; Officer Irvin had not placed her in handcuffs, but as he escorted her into the backseat of his locked police car, Meghan felt her stomach churn. Tears fell from her eyes, and she began making loud wheezing noises as she struggled to catch her breath.

"Are you okay back there?" Officer Irvin asked.

"Yes… yes, Officer Irvin," she yelped, trying to contain herself.

"Just call me Jack, that's easier," he said.

"I'm fine, Jack," she responded.

When they reached the Sandy Bay Police Station, Jack led Meghan into a small, windowless white room. Two thin iron chairs sat facing each other in the middle of the room, and Jack beckoned toward the one farther from the door.

"Have a seat," he ordered, and Meghan sank into the iron chair.

"I'm going to be asking you some questions regarding your relationship with Norman Butcher, as well as some general questions. You may have a lawyer present, if you wish. Would you like me to call your lawyer?"

Meghan shook her head, her body shaking in fear. "I'm innocent," she breathed. "Innocent people don't need lawyers. We can talk."

Jack nodded. "Good. I'll be recording you while we talk. Let's get started."

The questioning had gone late into the evening, and it was clear to Meghan that Jack believed she had killed Norman Butcher. He had been gentle at first during their interview, but afterwards, his tone became patronizing and rude.

"What do you mean, you just decided to open a bakery?" he had asked Meghan. "Who does that? You have no experience and you've never been to Sandy Bay, and you just happen to open a bakery? Doesn't that sound strange to you, Ms. Truman?"

Meghan tried to be polite, but as the hours wore on, she became more annoyed with Jack's attitude. She was innocent until proven guilty, and Jack was not treating her as though she were innocent.

"It all just doesn't add up to me," he said as Meghan stifled a yawn. "Why would some girl move up to Sandy Bay to start a bakery? With no experience and no family here, it just isn't making sense. But, from everything we've discussed, along with the tests run today, there isn't enough evidence to charge you with murder."

Meghan had sighed in relief, but Jack continued, "You won't be charged, but you will be watched. I will be stopping by with further questions as we continue to investigate, and I *strongly* encourage you not to even think of leaving this town until this mystery has been solved. Understood?"

Meghan frowned. Jack spoke to her as though she were a

petulant child. "Understood," she replied. She rose from her chair, and Jack led her to the lobby.

"Sweetie!"

Meghan heard Karen's familiar voice as she stepped across the threshold. Karen rushed to Meghan and hugged her. "I cannot *believe* this is happening. You poor thing."

Meghan leaned into Karen's embrace, thankful to have a friendly face amidst the police officers who looked at her with disdain.

"Excuse me? Where is her attorney? Was she allowed to call an attorney?" Meghan looked up and saw Debbie chastising Jack, who was shrugging his shoulders at the blonde woman angrily shaking a finger at him.

"Debbie called and told me you were here. I was so upset that I had her drive me," Karen admitted, pulling Meghan closer. "I thought it would be good to have someone else come with me to prove your innocence. It looks better to have more people around, and I'm so glad Debbie called."

Debbie walked over and raised an eyebrow at Meghan. "The officer says you refused an attorney because you're saying you're innocent. Not sure that's what I would have done, but I admire your thinking. Now, let's get out of here. We should really get you home, Meghan."

The next few days were the quietest Meghan had spent in Sandy Bay. While she had not been officially deemed a suspect, *everyone* knew that the police had taken her to the station, and Meghan did not have a single customer at Truly Sweet after Jack had shown up.

"I didn't do it," she lamented to Karen after Sally Sheridan had visited to demand her refund. "I couldn't do that. I didn't like the guy, but I would never *kill* anyone!"

Karen took Meghan's hand. "I know, sweetie," she said comfortingly. "You're a fabulous young woman, and this is an injustice. This is a small town, Meghan, and people always talk about new people, no matter how wonderful the new folks are. I *know* you didn't do it, and I would bet anything on your innocence."

Meghan looked sadly at Karen. "I don't know how I'm going to make it," she said, looking around the empty bakery. "I put all of my savings into this place, and now, I have no customers. Jack Irvin told me not to leave town, but if my name isn't cleared soon and the killer isn't found, then I'll be worse off than what I was back in LA."

Karen wrinkled her nose and adjusted her high ponytail. "Sweetie," she said softly. "Could you go home to Texas if this all doesn't work out? I would hate to see you go; you know how excited I am to have you here in Sandy Bay. I just don't want you to lose everything over some stupid apple pie."

Meghan thought for a moment. She feasibly *could* go home to Texas; her parents hadn't wanted her to move to California in the first place, and they would be thrilled if she came home.

"There's always Texas," she admitted. "But I never want to go back there. I finally got out. I lived in LA, and now, I'm in the Pacific Northwest. Texas is my past, not my future, Karen."

Karen shrugged. "I just don't know what to tell you, sweetie."

Meghan shook her head. "I've been through too much and given too much to this dream to just let it die," she said, her voice filled with determination and her hazel eyes sparkling. She flipped her dark hair behind her shoulder and held her head high. "I'm going to figure out who killed Norman Butcher. I'm going to clear my name and solve this mystery!"

Karen's eyes widened, but she grinned at Meghan and pumped her fist enthusiastically, as though she were at a zumba class instead of discussing a murder case.

"Way to go, Sweetie," Karen said. "That's the spirit!"

Meghan nodded. "And I know just who to talk to first," she said, biting her lower lip as she recounted her first and only visit to Norman's tea shop. "Lori Butcher knows something, and I'm going to find out what it is."

6

M eghan returned to truly sweet with sagging shoulders and a knot in her stomach. She had spent the last two hours grilling Lori, and as she unlocked the yellow door of the bakery, Meghan knew it had been a mistake.

"I really don't know anything!" Lori had cried as Meghan demanded information. "I found him, dead as a doornail, and that's all, Meghan."

Meghan had softened her tone upon seeing how upset Lori was, but the damage was done; Lori wept throughout their entire conversation, and the two-hour chat had yielded no new information for Meghan to process.

As Meghan stepped inside her bakery, the telephone rang. Meghan ran to answer it, and she heard a familiar male voice on the other end of the line.

"Meghan," Jack Irvin said in a business-like voice. "This is Jack Irvin with the Sandy Bay Police Department."

"I remember who you are. We spent *hours* together this week, Jack," she replied.

"Yes. Well, I want to advise you to stay away from Mr.

Butcher's tea shop. It isn't wise of you to be snooping around there, and I think you need to limit your activities as we continue our investigation."

Meghan nearly dropped the phone, looking around the bakery. "How did you know I was at the tea shop?" she asked, her voice shaking. "I just got home!"

"This is a small town, Meghan," he answered. "People talk. Keep that in mind."

The next morning, as Meghan dutifully prepared the kitchen, believing it best to proceed as normally as possible, she heard a knock at the front door.

"Please don't let Mrs. Sheridan be back," she muttered to herself as she walked to the door. She peered out of the window and found Debbie, Karen's niece, on her doorstep.

"What a surprise!" she said, throwing open the door and hugging Debbie. "I'm happy to see a friendly face."

Debbie smiled, stiff in Meghan's arms.

"Can we chat?" Debbie asked, looking around the quiet bakery. "My aunt mentioned that you are looking into the case yourself, and I think I have some information you might want."

Meghan's eyes lit up. "Please! Have a seat. You can see we're just *so* crowded here at Truly Sweet today."

Debbie gave Meghan a tight-lipped smile and sat in one of the white chairs. "I have the name of a suspect in the case," Debbie said quietly. "My lawyer, Vince Fisher? He and I were meeting to talk through some business, and he mentioned that he's been wrangled in to being Lori Butcher's attorney."

Meghan paled at Lori's name. "Lori Butcher?" she whispered. "But I talked with her myself. She didn't have anything to say about the case."

Debbie pursed her lips. "That isn't what Vince said. I may have pushed him a little; you know that I am interested in partnering in this business with you, and the financial gains from the bakery are in jeopardy if this murder doesn't get solved. Anyway, I pressed Vince, and he told me that Lori was caught *stealing* from Norman before he died."

Meghan leaned forward, engrossed in what Debbie was telling her. "Sweet Lori *stole* from Norman?"

Debbie nodded. "Apparently he hadn't paid Lori in *weeks*, and she lost her senses and *stole* from him instead of getting a lawyer. She needed money for food and to pay the rent back to Norman that he charged her, his own daughter! Vince told me that when Norman found out, he scolded her so badly in front of customers, and he even threatened to kick her out of the house."

Meghan gnashed her teeth, unsure of what to think about the new information.

"Anyway, Vince said to keep it under wraps, but I thought you should know."

With that, Debbie stood from her chair, gave Meghan a stiff hug, and scuttled out of the bakery.

"Lori stole from Norman because he mistreated her at home and at work," Meghan intoned to herself, trying to make sense of what Debbie had told her. "Lori is a suspect, too."

Later that day, the silver bells attached to the front door chimed, as Meghan's jaw clenched as Lori Butcher walked through the front door of Truly Sweet.

"Hi, Meghan," Lori said timidly, her hands pressed together in front of her waist. "Can we talk?"

Meghan nodded and pointed to one of the dainty white tables. "Have a seat. I'll get you something to eat." A flush crept up Lori's neck, and Meghan decided it would be unwise to give *anything* to another Butcher.

"What can I do for you, Lori?" she asked, taking a seat across from the nervous girl. Lori rocked back and forth, and she nibbled on her upper lip as Meghan stared at her.

"Lori?"

Lori took a deep breath. "Is that job still available?"

Meghan nearly let out a laugh at the audacity of Lori's question. "Lori," she answered with amusement. "I'm a suspect in your father's murder case. The police think I poisoned him. I know I didn't do it, and I hope you don't think I did. But regardless, I don't know if it's best that we spend time together right now, let alone work together."

Lori's face crumpled. "I need the job, Meghan," she whimpered. "My father is dead, and the funeral plans have been *so* expensive. I don't have access to all of his accounts and information, and without some help, I can't even afford to eat three meals a day."

Meghan's heart softened, and she saw the fear in Lori's eyes. "Lori," she said, racking her brain for a solution. "I have to think about it, and I need to talk with the police. There's so much going on right now, and I just don't know…."

"Please," Lori whispered, her eyes red and her shoulders sagging. "Please."

When Lori left moments later, Meghan immediately called Karen for advice. After explaining the odd visit from Lori, Karen offered Meghan some advice.

"The right thing to do would be to hire her," she said as Meghan groaned. "If she is really in need, then you'll be doing a good deed. And if she isn't… well… perhaps it's a good idea to keep her close by…"

"Don't do it, Meghan!"

Meghan heard Debbie in the background.

"Debbie's here, let me put her on speakerphone," Karen said as Meghan heard a click of buttons.

"Meghan, remember what we talked about when I visited? Lori *stole* from Norman! She's a *suspect*! Keeping her around is a terrible idea. You can't afford to hire her, either. As your self-appointed financial advisor, I am strongly encouraging you to disregard what my aunt is telling you and to not hire Lori."

"Oh, hush, you!" Karen said to Debbie. "You need to do more yoga. Yoga makes you kind and giving, which is what Meghan needs to be to Lori! Meghan, sweetie, hire Lori. You'll be helping her out, which is good karma for you, and you can keep an eye on *her*."

"Don't listen to her…." Debbie shrieked as the phone call cut off. Meghan wrung her hands together and took a deep breath.

"Being accused of murder one day, then hiring a murder suspect," Meghan murmured as she reached for the phone to dial Lori. "Who *knows* what will be next for Truly Sweet?"

7

Meghan stared into the mountain of whipped cream foam atop her large, whole milk, caramel mocha latte as she and Karen chatted away. Karen had shown up to take Meghan for girl talk and a cup of coffee, as they used to in LA, and both women were surprised when Debbie showed up.

"You just can't give up," Karen had been saying as Debbie marched in. "You're too fabulous to quit, Meghan. Believe in yourself."

"There you two are!" Debbie said. "I have some news for you," she announced, wagging her index finger at Meghan. "A little birdie told me that there *might* just be another suspect in this thing."

Meghan squeezed her eyes shut. She wasn't ready for another intense discussion about the case; she and Karen had been talking about the murder all morning at the coffee shop, and Debbie's interruption made Meghan anxious.

"Jamie Cruise. Have you met him? He's the handyman in town? Quiet? Kind of dirty? Anyway, rumor is that he had some gripes with Norman Butcher, and if you've seen Jamie, you *know* that he looks like he could kill."

Karen held up a hand, and her expression hardened. "Debbie!" Karen chastised. "I am *embarrassed* that any niece of mine would judge a book by its cover. Jamie Cruise is a good man; I used to babysit for him when I was a teenager, and I know he could never kill anyone. Who did you hear from that Jamie is a suspect?"

Debbie's face darkened. "I have my sources," she said, tossing her hair behind her back and raising her chin. "Anyway, I'm just saying it would be unwise to overlook Jamie Cruise. He's the perfect suspect, Meghan."

Meghan crossed her arms across her chest. "Jamie didn't kill Norman Butcher," she declared, shrugging her shoulders and leaning back in her seat. "I know he didn't."

Debbie raised both eyebrows, and her forehead wrinkled. "What do *you* know about Jamie Cruise?"

Meghan took a sip of her latte. "Lori Butcher told me who he was," she said, wiping the whipped cream from her upper lip as she finished her drink. "He was at the tea shop when I visited. Lori mentioned that he was a good handyman, and when I needed some things done around the bakery, I gave him a call."

Karen nodded. "He helped Meghan rewire the back ovens," she explained to Debbie. "He's been a fabulous help. Isn't he coming back by tomorrow to finish off the leak in the dishwasher, Meghan, dear?"

"He'll be by before ten," Meghan agreed, watching Debbie's face lose its color. "Debbie? Why are you fixated on Jamie?"

Debbie pursed her lips. "I just have a bad feeling about him," she explained. "Vince Fisher dropped some more information to me and mentioned that Norman hadn't been paid for some work he did at the tea shop. I think that sounds like a motive, don't you?"

Meghan's eyes widened, but Karen shook her head. "No," she stated, frowning at her niece. "I *know* Jamie Cruise and his family. He's a good man, Debbie. Come by tomorrow and see for yourself. He'll be by in the morning, and you can grill him all you want."

Debbie scowled as she rose from the table. "I'm just trying to help you," she insisted. "If Vince Fisher is giving me information, we should *use* it. Anyway, I'll see you both tomorrow."

Meghan and Karen watched as Debbie strode out of the coffee shop. "That was tense," Meghan said under her breath. "What's her deal?"

Karen rolled her eyes. "My niece can be uppity; she seems to dislike anyone who doesn't share her affinity for designer clothes and fancy things. I don't know what Vince Fisher thinks he's doing by dropping information to my niece, but her blaming Jamie Cruise is ridiculous. Jamie is a good man, and a little dirt on his boots didn't kill anyone."

The next morning, Jamie walked into the bakery only moments before Debbie came marching in.

"Good morning, Meghan. Karen, good to see you."

Karen reached to kiss Jamie's cheek. "Good morning to you, Jamie! How ya been?"

Jamie frowned. "Not real good," he admitted. "This Norman Butcher mess is causing a real stir around town, isn't it?"

Meghan watched Jamie's face for any indication of emotion; she felt it was strange that he had brought up the murder, and she wondered why he would discuss such a twisted event instead of making polite small talk.

"Is Debbie onto something?" Meghan thought to herself as Karen and Jamie chatted. "Did Jamie have something to do with Norman Butcher's death? It seems odd that he would instantly bring up the murder....I wonder..."

"Hello!"

Meghan turned to see Debbie walking through the front door, the silver bells chiming furiously.

"Aunt Karen. Meghan. Mr. Cruise. Hello!"

Jamie stiffened. "You can just call me Jamie," he said as he stared down at his shoes.

Debbie nodded. "Sure thing. Anyway, I hear that you're helping in the bakery today, Jamie?"

Jamie looked at Meghan and smiled. "She's been giving me some good business," he said, gesturing at Meghan. "She pays me *and* sends me home with treats! I can't complain about that."

Debbie took a step closer to Jamie, her eyebrow raised. "So, she pays you, huh? It's good to be paid, isn't it?"

Jamie cocked his head to the side. "Yes? Almost all of my customers in Sandy Bay have been good about paying me on time."

Debbie folded her arms at her side. "Almost?"

The color drained from Jamie's face. "This is about Mr. Butcher, isn't it?" he whispered. "I told the police that Norman hadn't paid me. He and I had some words the week before he died, but I wouldn't *kill* anyone over some late bills."

Karen glared at her niece. "Debbie, that is enough," she hissed.

"Now that you mention Norman Butcher, I'm just curious, Jamie," Debbie continued, disregarding Karen's furious expression. "Where were you at the time of the murder?"

Meghan gasped. Debbie's questioning was so direct; Meghan suspected it was from Debbie's years on the East Coast, but she felt uncomfortable as Debbie demanded answers from Jamie.

"I'll tell you what I told the police," he said, his eyes dark. "I was helping Kirsty Fisher prepare the convention center for the food festival this weekend. Just ask Kirsty."

Debbie breathed loudly out of her nose, but Meghan could see she was forcing herself to hold her smile. "Ahhh! How nice. Kirsty is such a dear."

"Aren't you taking food down to the food festival, Meghan?" Karen asked. "That'll be such a good way to rehabilitate your image and help Truly Sweet get back on top."

Meghan nodded. "A few days before the murder, Kirsty Fisher asked me to set up a booth. I know a lot has happened, but I haven't heard anything that suggests I'm disinvited so…."

"So you'll be there! How wonderful that will be." Karen declared.

"I might just give Kirsty Fisher a little call to check on your story," Debbie said, staring at Jamie. "The food festival is one of Sandy Bay's best events, and it seems a little strange that Kirsty would reach out to *you* for help."

Jamie shook his head. "I think I'm going to get out of here for today. I'll come back tomorrow, Meghan. Karen, good to see you. Goodbye, girls."

As Jamie walked out of Truly Sweet, Karen turned to Debbie. "How could you act like that?" she shouted. "Jamie is shy and kind, and you embarrassed him! He's working for *Meghan*, and you had no business being so rude, Debbie."

Debbie furrowed her brow. "I'm trying to help Meghan solve this murder, Aunt Karen!" she declared. "It's important that we talk to everyone involved, and Vince told me that Jamie was being watched."

Karen gritted her teeth. "Jamie just said he was with Vince's *wife*, Kirsty, during the murder. Did Vince mention *that* to you?"

"Well," Debbie sputtered. "He *may* have mentioned it, but

I wanted to talk to him, anyway. He's so filthy, and I just *know* that he's up to no good."

Karen and Debbie glowered at each other, and Meghan moved to stand between the two angry women. "Hey," Meghan said softly. "Let's all calm down. Debbie, it's sweet of you to care about my business and me, but I think we should just let the police take it from here. I don't want to hurt anyone's feelings, and I think Jamie felt bad while you talked to him this morning."

Debbie stared at Meghan. "But, Meghan," she pleaded. "It's your *business*! Do you want to lose it all? I'm just trying to help."

Karen fixed her eyes on her niece. "Debbie," she said sternly. "We're all going to back off for a bit and give this thing some time to settle. Poor Jamie was embarrassed and it's time we step back. The police are involved, and we need to let them do their jobs."

Debbie's eyes grew large. "Fine," she said after pausing for a moment. "We'll take a break. But keep in mind that the murderer is still on the loose. I just don't want to be the unlucky fool who gets killed next."

8

"Just keep moving," Meghan grunted to herself as she hauled herself forward on the running trail. "Breathe, move, head up."

Meghan had risen before sunrise to run, and now that she was nearly a mile into the workout, she was struggling to maintain her pace; it had been months since Meghan had put on her running shoes, but after a fitful night of sleep, she had set an early alarm in hopes that the run would clear her mind.

"Three miles left, three miles left," she chanted to herself as she swung her hips in rhythm with her steps.

As Meghan ran, she thought about her tumultuous time in Sandy Bay. She had *never* been at the center of any sort of scandal before; the only time Meghan Truman had ever been disliked was when she won a spot on the homecoming court her sophomore year in high school, making her then-best friend maddeningly jealous. The odd sensation of being scorned by the entire town in Sandy Bay was unfamiliar, and Meghan struggled to focus on her workout as she navigated the jogging path that cut through Sandy Bay Woods.

"Who could have killed Norman?" she thought to herself as her mind drifted from the pop playlist playing through her headphones. "Lori? Jamie? A disgruntled customer? Who could it have been?"

Meghan racked her brain for answers, but she couldn't think of anyone; she hardly knew anyone in Sandy Bay, and there was no obvious suspect, at least in her mind. She didn't think Lori had killed Norman; Lori was so timid and innocent, and while Meghan had no evidence to prove Lori didn't kill her father, Meghan's gut instinct told her to let Lori be.

Two miles into the run, Meghan's phone died, putting an end to the fast-paced, loud pop playlist she had been listening to.

"Ugh," she lamented, stuffing her phone in the pocket of her shorts. "I guess it's just me out here, then."

It *wasn't* just Meghan; as she pumped her arms and willed her aching legs to move, she heard the crackle of leaves behind her. The sun was beginning to rise, but an ominous fog covered the trail. Meghan glanced back, hearing the pounding of unfamiliar footsteps behind her, but as she tilted her head toward the noise, she saw no one.

"Weird," she thought, turning back to the path in front of her. The footsteps grew louder, and Meghan could sense the presence of another person. She jerked her head around, and out of the corner of her eye, she saw a dark figure looming behind her. Meghan began to sprint, forcing her feet to cycle faster and faster over the pavement, but the dark figure picked up speed as well.

Out of nowhere, Meghan's legs fell out from beneath her, and she tumbled to the ground. She started screaming as the black figure drew closer, and she reached for the towel and water bottle she had tucked into her shorts before leaving for her run. She reared back her arm and hurled the items at the dark figure, howling in fear as she realized she was completely alone.

As the water bottle hit the dark figure, Meghan continued to scream. The dark figure stopped only feet from Meghan, turning around to run in the direction they had both come from. Meghan heard a small clink as the dark figure disappeared into the darkness of the early morning, and she stood from her place on the pavement.

"Ouch," she whimpered, feeling a sharp pain in her ankle. She hobbled to where the stalker had stopped. On the pavement was a familiar-looking key, and Meghan picked it up to examine it.

"What is this?" Meghan whispered. She squinted, looking at the small key.

"Hey!"

Meghan turned around and found Jack Irvin staring at her. He was dressed in running attire, and a panting dog sat dutifully at his feet.

"What are you doing out here? It's practically the middle of the night." Jack said, looking quizzically at Meghan as she surreptitiously tucked the key into her pocket.

"Same thing you're doing, I guess," she said, her heart still pounding from the encounter with the dark figure. She thought about mentioning the dark figure to Jack, but decided against it; she knew Jack was leery of her, and she didn't want to make him even more suspicious with talk of a strange, dark figure in the woods. "I wanted to get a run in."

"Seems a little strange to be out here at this time," he said.

"Running helps me clear my head, and I needed some time to think," she responded.

Jack tilted his head to the side, but said nothing. Meghan reached down to pet his dog.

"Cute puppy! What's her name?" she asked, scratching the dog's neck.

"Dash. He's a boy," he answered curtly, still giving Meghan a strange look. "What happened there?" Jack pointed to Meghan's ankle.

She looked down and gasped. Her ankle had swollen significantly; the skin visible over her white socks was bulging and red, and she could feel the area throbbing.

"Sit, Dash," he ordered the dog. Dash sat down on the pavement, his tail wagging, and his eyes tracking his owner. "Meghan, you sit down, too."

"You're off duty, *Officer Irvin*," she responded. "You don't have to give me orders."

Jack shrugged. "Your ankle is injured, and it looks like you need some help. Let me look at it."

Meghan lowered herself to the ground, and Jack kneeled next to her. Meghan could feel the heat radiating from his body; it was a warm morning, and he had clearly been running quickly before finding her on the path.

"Let me just…." he said, tenderly removing Meghan's sock and shoe to examine her ankle. "Yeah, it's not broken, but it's definitely sprained. I don't live too far away….why don't I help you back to my place? I can ice it up, and then I can drive you home."

Meghan paused, but after a jolt of pain shot up her leg, she nodded. "Thanks, that would be great."

Jack helped her up and guided her arm around his muscular shoulders. "It's only a short walk from here," he said, and Meghan shivered as her bare arms touched his.

Jack helped Meghan limp to his house. "This is it," he said as they arrived outside a small, one-story green house on the edge of the woods. "The Irvin Estate."

Jack held open the front door for Meghan and guided her to the couch. "Sit," he said.

"I'm *not* a dog," she said. "No need to order me about, *Officer*."

Jack laughed. "I'm trying to help you out, Meghan," he said, retrieving a bag of frozen peas from his refrigerator. "Relax."

Meghan shifted awkwardly on the couch. "It's hard to relax when you're sitting on the couch of someone who thinks you're a murderer," she muttered, looking down at her swollen ankle.

"What did you say?" he said sharply. "I don't think that was called for."

Meghan rolled her eyes. "I don't think the way you treated me at the station was called for," she said. "I was clearly upset, and by law, I'm *innocent* until proven guilty, which is not how you acted when you interrogated me!"

Jack placed the frozen peas on Meghan's ankle and held the bag there for several long, tense minutes.

"Well, thanks for your help," she said, no longer able to stand the awkward silence as Jack iced her ankle. "I'll just see myself out."

Jack stood up and gestured toward the kitchen. "Look," he said, his face sincere. "I'm sorry. I was a bit harsh when we talked at the station, and I should have been more professional. Let me make it up to you. Stay for breakfast. Word on the street is that my fried eggs are the best in Sandy Bay!"

Meghan giggled. "Fried eggs? *Anyone* can make fried eggs. I bet Dash can make fried eggs."

Dash wagged his tail at the mention of his name, and Meghan patted to the spot on the couch beside her. "Here, boy! Come!" Dash leaped onto the couch and made himself at home on Meghan's lap. "Good boy." she whispered, stroking Dash's soft chest.

Jack shook his head. "No, no. You haven't had fried eggs until you've had mine. Stay. I'll make you a killer breakfast, and then you can hobble on with your day."

Meghan laughed again. "You're funny for someone who

thinks I'm a murderer," she said, leaning back onto the couch, relaxing for the first time all day.

"Too soon for jokes," he said, but Meghan could see the handsome smile on his face as he opened the kitchen cabinets and began making breakfast for her.

"Just my luck," Meghan thought to herself as Jack started to whistle. She forced the thoughts of the dark stranger in the woods from her mind while watching Jack's bulging biceps as he reached for a pan. "A handsome police officer is making breakfast for me. Maybe things are *finally* going to get better in Sandy Bay." She drank in the sparse but tasteful furnishing in Jack's abode, and for the first time in a long time, Meghan forced herself to relax.

9

"**A**nd just *where* have you been, Meghan Truman?" Karen asked as Meghan limped into the bakery after her breakfast with Jack.

"Karen!" Meghan exclaimed. "What are you doing here?"

Karen gave Meghan an amused look. "I told you I was stopping by after my pilates class," she said. "I let myself in with the key you gave me."

At the mention of a key, Meghan slipped her hand in her pocket, feeling the small, cold key the dark figure had dropped in the woods. She thought about mentioning the scary incident to Karen, but decided against it, at least for the moment; Meghan was brimming with excitement after the hour spent with Jack, and she wanted to revel in the magic of her morning with Karen, *not* discuss murderers and dark figures.

"So? Meghan Truman, you are blushing. Was that Jack Irvin's police car I saw dropping you off?"

Meghan grinned.

"Well! Sit down and tell me *everything*," Karen insisted,

pulling out one of the white chairs. "Tell me everything, including what happened to your leg. Why are you limping? You look worse than I did two years ago after my marathon in Lisbon, and you're still young."

Meghan explained she had been restless and gone for a jog, and after hurting herself, Jack and his dog had discovered her in the woods. "He took me back to his house, iced my leg, and made breakfast for me."

"Sounds like someone had a good morning." Karen said, winking at Meghan.

The two women visited for a while longer. After Karen left, Meghan slowly made her way upstairs. She was overcome with exhaustion after her night of poor sleep, and while she had stifled her shock during her encounter with Jack, the situation with the dark figure had thoroughly scared Meghan.

"That could not have been a coincidence," Meghan thought to herself as she snuggled into her bed. "What are the odds that a stranger would just randomly follow me? Maybe someone knows that I've been digging around and trying to find Norman's killer. Maybe the wrong person knows what I'm up to...."

Meghan began to drift off to sleep, but before she slipped into unconsciousness, she thought of Jack. He had been so kind to make breakfast for her, and Meghan felt her face grow warm as she recalled their time together.

"I have to prove to Jack that I'm innocent..." she thought as she finally surrendered to the thick, comfortable tug of sleep.

The next morning, as Meghan swept the kitchen, Lori Butcher walked through the front door.

"Good morning, Meghan!" Lori said, smiling softly at Meghan. "I wanted to stop by and see if you had decided on that job?"

Meghan took a deep breath. She hadn't thought much about Lori in the last twenty-four hours; between the dark figure and breakfast with Jack, Meghan's mind had been racing, and she had not definitively decided on giving the job to Lori.

"Ooops!" Lori said, pulling Meghan from her thoughts. Lori had spilled the contents of her purse on the floor. Meghan kneeled to help Lori pick up her things.

"Lori?" she said slowly as she spotted a small key on the wooden floor of the bakery. "Is this yours?"

Lori nodded. "That's the key to my apartment," she said, taking it from Meghan's hands. "Thanks! I lost my spare, and I wouldn't be able to get in without this."

Meghan's heart started pounding. The key was identical to the one dropped by the dark figure.

"Hey, Lori?" she asked, trying to maintain her composure as she stood up from the floor and backed away from Lori. "Are you a morning person?"

Lori shook her head vigorously. "Oh, no. I sleep in almost every morning. My best shifts at the tea shop are the noon to close shifts. I'm useless before noon."

Meghan tightened her jaw. "What were you doing at six yesterday morning?"

Lori laughed. "I was sleeping!" she said. "Why?"

"Are you sure you weren't following me at Sandy Bay Woods?"

Lori's eyes widened. "What?"

Meghan narrowed her eyes at Lori. "Just tell me, Lori. Did you follow me yesterday? Did you *kill* Norman Butcher?"

"No!" she said, her face pale. "Why would you ask me that, Meghan?"

Not wanting to reveal to Lori that she had the matching key, Meghan gulped, forcing a smile on her lips. "I'm just being silly," she said, biting her cheeks to widen her grin. "Of *course* you were sleeping in. I believe you, Lori."

Meghan did *not* believe Lori, but she wasn't ready to play all of her cards, *or* her keys, at least not yet.

10

"**M**eghan! Meghan! Wake up! Meghan!"

Meghan sat up in bed and glanced at her alarm clock. It was nearly three in the morning. Who could possibly be shouting for her in the middle of the night? The yelling was coming from outside, and Meghan rubbed her eyes as she lumbered to the window.

"Meghan! Meghan!"

Meghan raised her window and peered outside. Lori Butcher, clad in a set of yellow pajamas, was jumping up and down.

"Meghan! Someone was in my room trying to strangle me! It must be the person who killed my father!"

Meghan gasped. "I'll be right down," she called down to Lori. Meghan slipped on her running shoes and ran downstairs, wincing at the shooting pain in her ankle, but knowing that she had to hurry.

"Lori," Meghan said when she made it downstairs. "Get inside." Lori stepped inside the bakery, and Meghan bolted the door shut behind them.

"What happened?"

"Someone was trying to strangle me. I woke up with a pair of hands around my neck. I couldn't tell who it was; they were wearing dark clothes. I kicked them off of me, and they followed me downstairs. They were so quick, Meghan, but I made it outside and out of the house."

Meghan saw Lori was shaking, and she gently patted Lori's shoulder. "You couldn't tell who it was?" she asked, thinking of the dark figure who had followed her in the park.

"No," Lori said, her voice quivering. "I don't know who it was. I couldn't see their face, and their clothes were plain."

Meghan looked around the bakery, fearful that they were being watched. "We need to get out of here," she said authoritatively. "Let me make a call."

Twenty minutes later, Meghan and Lori were safely nestled in Karen's guest bedroom. After telling Karen what had happened to Lori, Karen insisted on picking them up in her orange jeep and taking them back to her house.

"You'll feel safer there," Karen assured Meghan over the phone. "Chief Nunan, one of the bigwigs at the Sandy Bay Police Department, is my neighbor. You'll feel much better with her nearby."

"Thanks, Karen," Meghan said, trying to stay calm.

"You have a busy day tomorrow. You need your sleep."

"The food festival," Meghan said, hitting herself on the forehead with her palm. "I forgot!"

"You need to go, Meghan. You said it yourself that by being in the food festival, you can repair your image and help Truly Sweet. Look, I'll come get you two, you can sleep soundly, and then, Lori can help you with the food festival. It'll be fabulous. Just hold tight, now; I'll be over in three minutes."

The next morning, Karen woke Meghan and Lori in time to set up for the food festival.

"I just got back from the most fabulous fifteen mile jog,

ladies!" Karen said gleefully as she peered into the guest bedroom. "The sun is shining, and it's a gorgeous day. Rise and shine! You two have a lot to do."

Karen dropped Meghan and Lori off at the food festival, and as they were setting up the Truly Sweet booth, Debbie stopped by.

"Meghan!" she said warmly. "The booth looks adorable."

Meghan smiled, happy that Debbie was in a better mood than when they had last spoken. "Thank you so much, Debbie," she replied, putting the finishing touches on the booth. "Good to see you. You know Lori Butcher?"

"Lori," Debbie said sweetly. "Lovely to see you. Anyway, Meghan? Do you need any help? I'm about to run to my karate class; I have a yellow belt exam today and have to run, but if you need anything in town, I could easily swing back by."

"That is so nice of you to offer." Meghan said, leaning over to hug Debbie. She paused, noticing several large bruises.

"Debbie!" she said, eyeing Debbie's thin arm. "What's on your arm?"

"Oh, it's nothing," Debbie said nonchalantly, tugging her sleeve down to cover her bruised forearms. "Karate gets the best of me sometimes; I want to be active like Aunt Karen, but I just don't have the athleticism she does, you know?"

Meghan nodded and pointed down to her swollen ankle. "I hear you."

Debbie chuckled. "Anyway, I must be off. Call me if you need anything; like I said, I'm happy to swing back by if you need anything from town."

"Good luck on your exam!" Meghan called as Debbie waved goodbye.

"She is the most ambitious person I've ever met," she said to Lori in admiration. "She's a little overbearing at times, but

I'm happy to have her on my team. She's one of the few *real* friends I have in Sandy Bay."

With that, Meghan tied a tidy yellow bow on the front of her booth.

"We're food festival ready," Meghan said, grinning at her handiwork. "Time to show the people of Sandy Bay that Truly Sweet is just that: truly sweet!"

11

"Thank goodness you are here!" Meghan said, relieved to see Karen's shiny purple sneakers moving through the crowd toward her. "I forgot the boxes of strudel. I brought ten cases of apple pies, and no one is touching them. I think if I run home to grab the strudel, I'll have more success."

Meghan and Lori had been minding the Truly Sweet booth for two hours, and while some passersby stopped to chat, once they realized who Meghan was, they walked along without making a purchase.

"I don't quite trust Lori," Meghan whispered to Karen as she watched Lori out of the corner of her eye. "Can you watch the booth while I run to the bakery? I won't be gone for more than fifteen minutes."

Karen nodded emphatically. "Of course. You run home. I'll take care of things here."

"Thanks, Karen." she said as she fetched her keys and purse.

When Meghan arrived at Truly Sweet, she realized the

yellow front door was slightly ajar. "That's odd," she said to herself as she stepped inside. "Hello? Is anyone there?

Meghan walked through the dining area and back to the kitchen. Her heart was pounding as she walked through the doors. Her eyes widened as she spotted a familiar figure.

"What are you doing here?" Meghan asked, lifting her hands to her hips. "You aren't supposed to be in here."

Debbie was huddled over the boxes of strudel, a bottle in her hands. She straightened up when she saw Meghan and flashed her brilliant white smile.

"What are you doing?" she repeated. "What are you putting in the strudel?"

Debbie held out the bottle so Meghan could see. "Rat poison?" she whispered. "You're putting rat poison in my desserts?"

"You caught me," Debbie said matter-of-factly. "It was me."

Meghan's jaw dropped. "Debbie, why? Why would you do this?"

"I hate not being the very best," she replied. "When you didn't make me a partner in your bakery, I couldn't stand the thought of this place making it, at least not without *me*."

Meghan's chin quivered. "A partner? But you never…"

"I made myself abundantly clear," she said, her eyes dancing with rage. "I also couldn't stand my aunt liking someone more than me. I'm the closest thing she has to a daughter, not you, and I'm so sick of hearing about *fabulous Meghan* and her *fabulous* desserts!"

Meghan's shoulders shook, and she took a step back from Debbie.

"Debbie," she whispered. "Why did you kill Norman?"

"Norman's always bothered me, but I didn't mean to kill him," she said. "I wanted Lori gone; Karen has always been too nice to Lori, and I hoped that poisoned pie would kill *her*.

I stole a key from their stupid tea shop, and it was all too easy to slip a dessert into their house. It was an accident that Norman ended up a goner."

Meghan felt the tears well in her eyes. "You killed him, Debbie, and you wanted *me* to take the fall?"

"Why do you think I was so invested in the investigation? Of course I wanted you to be blamed! I want you gone and out of the way. I don't think it's too late for that, either." Debbie reached for a sharp knife resting in the rack beside her.

"And it was you who was following me that morning in the park when I was jogging."

"It's good to know you can still think clearly despite all those desserts you make and consume."

"And poor ol' Lori…"

"That little goody two-shoes gets on my last nerves. I envisaged a total fresh start for Truly Sweet."

Meghan felt an equal measure of pity and outrage at Debbie as she spewed forth more diabolical venom from her lips.

"No one will care that Meghan Truman died," Debbie said venomously as she pointed the knife at Meghan. "This isn't your town. You're just a stranger here."

Meghan reached behind her for anything that would save her. She felt a bag of flour, and she tore it open with her fingernails, reaching into the bag and retrieving a handful of the white, fluffy powder.

"Take that!" Meghan shouted, throwing the powder in Debbie's eyes to blind her.

"Ahhh!" Debbie screeched. "Stop!" Debbie grabbed a sack of sugar and tossed it at Meghan. It hit Meghan directly in the stomach, and the breath was knocked out of her.

"Ooooof," Meghan said, losing her balance and falling

into a carton of eggs. She tried to get up, but her swollen ankle was stinging. Beads of sweat pooled at her hairline.

"Not so fast," Debbie said, appearing out of the white, dusty powder. "There's only room in this town for *one* fabulous lady, and that lady is *me!*"

Debbie raised the knife above her head, grasping the handle with both hands. She stepped on Meghan's chest, pinning Meghan to the ground.

"Bye, Meghan," she said, lowering the knife with immense force. Meghan closed her eyes to brace herself.

"THAT'S ENOUGH!"

There was a loud crash, and Meghan heard a familiar voice. She held her breath. The knife had not sunk into her body, and Meghan waited for the inevitable sharp pain.

"THAT IS ENOUGH, DEBBIE!"

Meghan opened her eyes. Debbie was lying on the floor across the room, and Karen was standing above her with a frying pan in her hands. The knife was on the floor beside Meghan, and she breathed a sigh of relief.

"I didn't want to believe you could do this," Karen shrieked, waving the pan above Debbie's head as Debbie moaned. "But when Lori told me about the intruder at her house, and Jamie Cruise mentioned that he's seen *you* walk into this bakery after-hours on more than one occasion, I just *knew* something was off."

Debbie reached up and cradled her head in her hands, groaning as Karen continued. "When Meghan told me you were at karate class today, I knew you were up to something.

Karate? Really? My fancy pants niece wouldn't go near a karate studio."

Debbie curled into a fetal position, saying nothing as Karen screamed at her. "And you try to stab Meghan? *My* Meghan? How could you? I knew the second I saw your car outside that something was wrong, and the police are on their way. I don't know what you've been up to, Debbie, but I'm *ashamed* to be your aunt!"

Meghan could see the tears spilling from Debbie's eyes, but she felt her stomach churn in disgust.

"You're done, Debbie," Karen barked. "You couldn't make it on Wall Street, and you couldn't make it as a murderer. *That's it!*"

The police arrived five minutes later, and as they led Debbie out in handcuffs, she pleaded with Karen. "Please," she wailed, pawing at her aunt. "Please don't let them take me. This was an accident. This was a misunderstanding. Please!"

Karen's eyes were cold as Debbie was taken away, and she shrugged. "Prison will be good for a fancy pants like you," she said. "You'll look just *fabulous* in orange."

"How's that ankle?"

Meghan looked up and blushed as Jack Irvin walked into Truly Sweet. The bakery was brimming with customers; ever since Debbie had confessed and Meghan's name had been officially cleared, business at Truly Sweet had never been better. Meghan felt her stomach flutter as Jack winked at her.

"It's feeling a lot better, thanks," she said, brushing her dark hair off of her shoulders and slowly lowering her eyelids.

"Meghan! Meghan, can you grab a piece of apple pie for table two?" Lori chirped as she emerged from the kitchen, her hands filled with clean plates. Meghan grinned; Lori had been working full time at the bakery for nearly a week now, and Meghan loved having her around. Lori was an excellent pastry chef, and her recipes complemented what Meghan already had on the menu.

"Give me a second, Lori," she said, turning to give Lori an excited look. "Officer Irvin just stopped by."

Jack groaned playfully. "*Jack*," he said. "It's *Jack*! I'm off duty!"

Meghan giggled. "But he isn't!"

Dash was sitting at Jack's feet, his tail wagging and his tongue out. "That boy needs a treat! Hi, Dash!"

Meghan came around to the front of the counter and leaned down to pet the dog. "Good boy!"

Jack grinned. "I think someone has a new favorite spot in town," he said as Meghan fed Dash a piece of peach crumble. "Don't give him too much."

Meghan rolled her eyes. "Yes, *Officer*," she said, winking at Jack. "You know, now that I think about it, you can't boss me around in my own bakery."

Jack raised an eyebrow. "What about outside of the bakery? Can I be bossy toward you somewhere else?"

Meghan smirked. "You seem to manage being bossy with me *everywhere* else," she said.

Jack thought for a moment. "What about at La Spezia, the Italian restaurant in town," he said cautiously, studying Meghan's face. "Could I be bossy toward you there?"

Meghan's face turned red, but she nodded. "Sure," she said, trying to stay cool. "You know what, Jack? I think that would be truly sweet."

The last few weeks had been chaotic, but Meghan was glad everything was falling into place. Sandy Bay was loving her, and she was loving it.

The End

Thank you for reading Apple Pie and Trouble. I really hope you enjoyed reading it as much as I had writing it!

If you have a minute, please consider leaving a review on Amazon, GoodReads and/or Bookbub.

Many thanks in advance for your support!

BROWNIES AND DARK SHADOWS

CHAPTER 1 SNEEK PEEK

ABOUT BROWNIES AND DARK SHADOWS

Released: July, 2018
Series: Book 2 – Sandy Bay Cozy Mystery Series
Standalone: Yes
Cliff-hanger: No

When Sandy Bay's crème de la crème congregate to raise money for charity, Meghan Truman is proud to have her tasty desserts the talk of the party. She's not so proud when the wealthiest couple in Sandy Bay are discovered dead and rumors circulate around town that her brownies are the cause of this tragedy.

This murder case casts a dark shadow over Meghan's budding romance with handsome Officer Irvin who's disappointed that she's once again at the center of another murder investigation.

With everything to lose, Meghan must work hard to clear her name, restore broken relationships and solve this murder mystery before everything she's worked so hard to build comes crumbling down.

CHAPTER 1 SNEEK PEEK

"**I** cannot *believe* we booked the Weeks Group corporate order!" Lori squealed, her eyes dancing with excitement.

Meghan smiled warmly at Lori. It had been a pleasant surprise to book such a lucrative deal; the Weeks Group was one of the largest companies on the West Coast, and Meghan knew what an honor it was for her bakery, Truly Sweet, to be chosen as the official bakery of the company. The bakery hadn't even been open for a year yet, and already, Meghan's business was the talk of the town!

"Just think, Meghan! Every restaurant and cafe at the Weeks Group will be filled with *your* sweets!" Lori exclaimed.

Meghan smiled down at Lori, her new assistant. Lori had only been working as Meghan's assistant for a few weeks, but Meghan adored Lori's warmth and enthusiasm. As the two women tied their aprons in the bakery's backroom and prepared for the day ahead, Meghan's heart swelled with gratitude for her protégé.

"*Our* sweets, Lori," Meghan gently corrected, placing a hand softly on Lori's shoulder. "You are my assistant now, Lori! You are a member of the team here. My success is *our* success, and I want you to know how proud I am of how quickly you've learned about the way I do things here at Truly Sweet!"

Lori beamed, her youthful face glowing with Meghan's kind words. At twenty-two, she was only a few years younger than Meghan, but her earnest spirit made her seem even younger than her age. Meghan enjoyed Lori's company, and she was thankful to have a new friend in her adopted hometown; Meghan had only recently moved to Sandy Bay, and with every kindred spirit found, she felt even more at home.

Meghan tucked a loose strand of dark hair behind her ear and finished tying her apron. She walked to the large sink in the backroom and washed her hands, careful to scrub every inch.

"Do we have a busy day today, Meghan?" Lori asked, wiping her own damp hands on her apron as she walked into the front room. Meghan shook her head.

"No," Meghan replied. "I received the call about the Weeks Group corporate order last night, and I went ahead and cleared our schedule for the week so that we can begin preparing! It will be an ongoing order, and I expect it will keep us busy. We'll have a few miscellaneous orders to fill this week, and surely some walk-in customers, but otherwise, it will be a quiet week!"

Meghan had barely finished her sentence before the bakery was abuzz with activity; suddenly, the tiny silver bells attached to the front door chimed as the door burst open. A petite, blonde-haired woman marched up to the front counter, the two strands of milky-white pearls around her neck jingling as she moved.

"Meghan Truman! You are *just* the person I need to speak with!"

Meghan's eyes widened as Kirsty Fisher sauntered up to the counter. Her heart sank; Kirsty was one of Sandy Bay's more influential residents, and she had acted aloof toward Meghan since the scandal that had threatened Truly Sweet's success only weeks ago. Kirsty had hardly acknowledged Meghan since the murder of Norman Butcher, a local man, had been blamed on Meghan and her treats. Even though Meghan's name had been cleared for weeks now, Kirsty's attitude had still been chilly. Meghan felt her hands quiver as Kirsty approached, and she bit her bottom lip nervously as Kirsty's lips turned upward into a business-like smile.

"Lori," Meghan hissed under her breath, trying to capture the attention of her trusted assistant who was rolling out dough behind her. Lori heard Meghan's whisper and immediately came to her side.

"Well, good morning, Kirsty!" Lori said kindly to the woman as she wiped her messy hands on her apron. "What brings you in this morning?"

Meghan's shoulders dropped in relief; a lifetime resident of Sandy Bay, Lori knew how to interact with *everyone* in town, and Meghan was thankful for her help as Kirsty eyed her.

Kirsty nodded at Lori, but quickly moved her attention back to Meghan.

"Meghan, dear! So lovely to see you. I hope you are well?"

Meghan shrugged nervously, and Kirsty continued.

"So Meghan, I've heard you bake the *best* brownies in town! Your bakery was the talk of the town over the last few weeks, you know, with… everything… that happened?"

Meghan watched as Lori disappeared into the backroom. The scandal had involved Lori; it was her father that had been murdered, and while he and Lori had not had a close relationship, Meghan knew Lori was still recovering from the loss.

"Anyway, I'm *so* terribly sorry that your first few weeks in Sandy Bay were tainted with such a scandal! How awful. This is such a lovely town, and I don't want you to get the wrong idea of us!" Kirsty said, her smile shifting into a look of concern.

Meghan shook her head. "It's alright," she replied. "My bakery's reputation has been restored, and I think things have settled down."

Kirsty gave Meghan a pitying smile.

"Well, I heard that your name was cleared. That's so wonderful. I just had a little idea that could help completely eliminate *any* more issues you may have been having because of that horrible little scandal!" Kirsty said, tossing her blonde hair behind her shoulders and retrieving a business card from her purse. "As you know, I run the Fisher Foundation, the biggest charity in town. We raise money for those in need, and it's nearly time for our annual gala, the Fisher Fest! My caterer unexpectedly canceled, and the new caterer will not be providing desserts. Since you are in need of some positive exposure in town, especially given that tricky little incident with Mr. Butcher, I thought it might be nice if you could provide some desserts for the gala!"

Meghan stared at Kirsty, her hazel eyes growing large. She took a long, silent breath, considering Kirsty's proposal.

"Well?" Kirsty asked, beginning to tap her high heels impatiently on the wooden floor.

"I don't know," Meghan finally answered. "I just took on a major corporate order, and I don't know if I have the time to make even more brownies with the commitment I just made."

Kirsty pursed her lips in a pout and batted her eyelashes at Meghan.

"Come on," Kirsty coaxed, sliding her business card across the counter. "Think about your business! This would quiet all the people still whispering about Truly Sweet, and you would have so many of Sandy Bay's finest folks sampling *your* treats at the gala!"

Meghan placed her hands on her round hips as she mentally calculated the hours she would need to bake enough desserts to take to the gala. She knew that with Lori's help, she could do it, but for some reason, she felt uneasy about accepting Kirsty's proposal.

"Meghan?" Kirsty said sternly. "I need to know if you will help us! It's for *charity*. You simply cannot turn down the opportunity to bake for a *charity*!"

"Okay," Meghan answered, folding her hands in front on her. "I'll do it."

"Excellent!" Kirsty said gleefully, snapping her purse closed and stepping back from the counter. "Here's my card. Give me a call this evening and we'll work out the details. I think you might even thank me later, Meghan! Toodles!"

As Kirsty marched out of the bakery, her tall, thin high heels clacking across the floor, Meghan leaned back against the counter.

"What did she want?" Lori asked as she walked back into the front room. "Kirsty Fisher *always* wants something; she and her husband run every event and charity in town, and no one can say no to Kirsty Fisher."

Meghan shrugged. "We're baking for the Fisher Fest," she said to Lori. Lori's eyes sparkled as she heard the news.

"The Fisher Fest!" Lori exclaimed. "That's the fanciest event all year! Kirsty even makes the caterers and workers dress up! We'll have so much fun, Meghan! This is good news!"

Meghan looked down at her shoes, her chest feeling tight.

"Meghan? This is good news! Between the Weeks Group

deal and the Fisher Fest, things are looking up for Truly Sweet!"

Meghan shook her head. "I don't know what's wrong with me," Meghan whispered. "I just have a bad feeling about this event. For some reason, Fisher Fest has me worried, Lori."

* * *

You can order your copy of **Brownies and Dark Shadows** at any good online retailer.

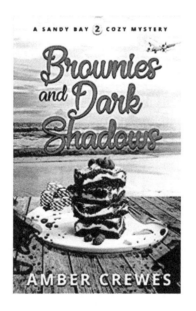

Made in the USA
Monee, IL
30 April 2023